To my parents, who encouraged me
to sing and dance and follow my own path.
—D.M.

To Mum & Dad, for always accepting me
and seeing me for who I am.
—R.C.

Clarion Books is an imprint of HarperCollins Publishers.

Free to Be Fabulous
Text copyright © 2024 by David McMullin
Illustrations copyright © 2024 by Robbie Cathro

Library of Congress Control Number: 2023943297
ISBN 978-0-06-323968-5

The artist used Procreate on iPad to create the digital illustrations for this book.
The text was set in Metallophile Sp8 and MonsterFonts - House of Terror.
Handletterings by Robbie Cathro
Interior design by Phil Caminiti

24 25 26 27 28 RTLO 10 9 8 7 6 5 4 3 2 1

First Edition

FREE to Be FABULOUS!

written by
DAVID MCMULLIN

illustrated by
ROBBIE CATHRO

CLARION BOOKS
An Imprint of HarperCollinsPublishers

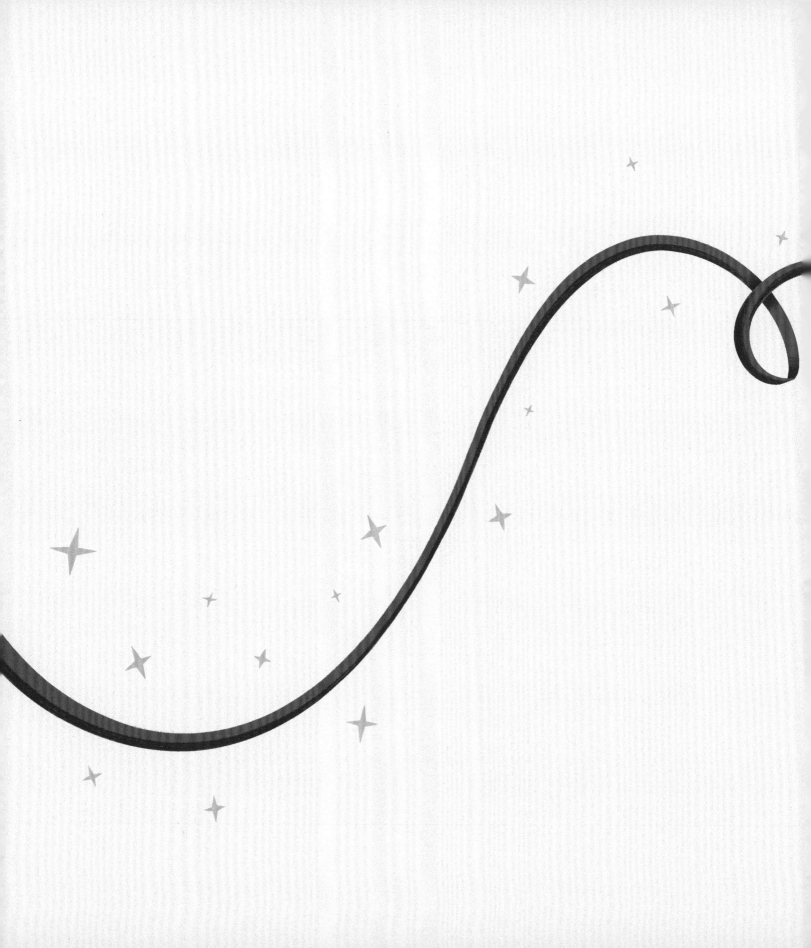

Daniel flipped for everything Fabulina!

In his room, they danced together to her biggest hit,

"STRONG, BRAVE, FREE."

With Fabulina, he could do anything.

When he got to school on the day of the talent show sign-ups,
Daniel knew exactly what he wanted to do.

"Is it okay if I dance?"

"I was hoping you would," said Mr. Edwards.

After school,

Daniel rehearsed.

Designed.

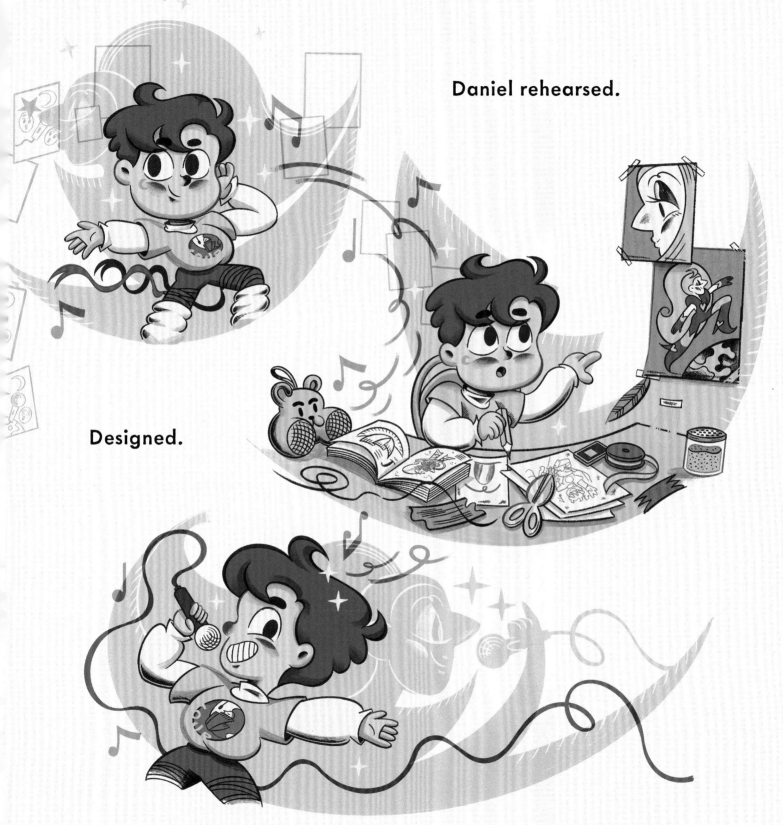

And prepared.

Finally, the day of the talent show arrived.

It was Daniel's turn when
"Strong, Brave, Free"
started to play.

Daniel blazed into the spotlight!

Every spin, leap, and shimmy kick was flawlessly Fabulina.

And as Daniel struck his final pose,
the audience leapt out of their seats.

At the very end of the talent show, Mr. Edwards announced the winner . . .

Daniel felt so much joy!

But then . . .

. . . **The Mean** noticed.

Maybe it would be best if he never shimmy kicked again.

But **The Mean** persisted.

So finally, Daniel hid.

"Daniel, why aren't you out celebrating your victory? You made quite a splash today."

"A *splash*? Is that good or bad?"
Daniel asked.

"Look out the window."

Daniel couldn't believe his eyes.
From one end of the playground to the other . . .

...DANCING

The kids. The teachers. Even the principal.

t was . . .

. . FABULOUS!

Maybe
if he sneaked out quietly,
The Mean
wouldn't notice.

He kept himself small and quiet
as he made his way outside.

"Look, it's Daniel!"

A group of kids gathered around him.
"We need your help."
Daniel let out a long breath. "My help?"

Daniel shared all of his favorite Fabulina moves.

Their dancing sparkled.

With fantastic Fabulina flair, he blazed into the spotlight once again.

But then **The Mean**
barreled in louder than ever!

Everyone backed away.
Daniel knew what to do.

Every spin, leap, and shimmy kick was flawlessly Fabulina.

He topped it off with some razzle-dazzle all his own—

DARINGLY DANIEL!

Daniel couldn't hear **The Mean** over the singing and cheering.

The Mean grew . . .

. . . quieter . . .

. . . and quieter until
no one paid it any attention.

Daniel strutted down the hallway. **"STRONG!"**

"BRAVE!"

And when he struck a pose,
Daniel felt . . .

"FREE!"